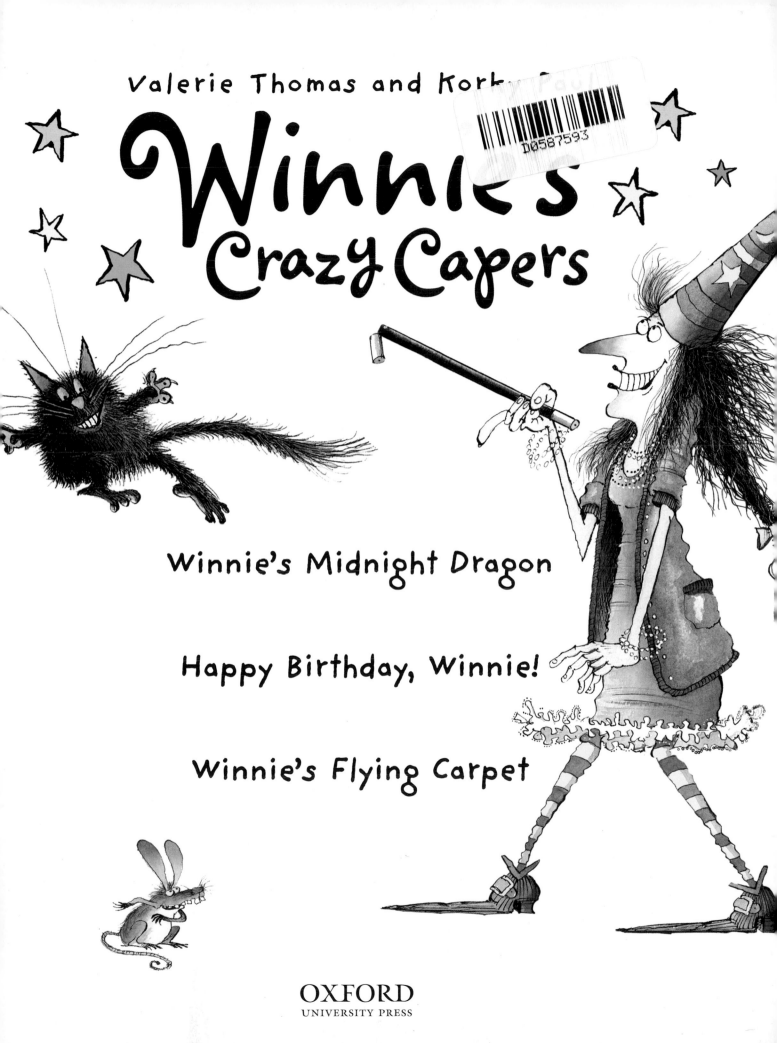

Valerie Thomas and Korky Paul

Winnie's Crazy Capers

Winnie's Midnight Dragon

Happy Birthday, Winnie!

Winnie's Flying Carpet

OXFORD
UNIVERSITY PRESS

OXFORD
UNIVERSITY PRESS

Great Clarendon Street, Oxford OX2 6DP
Oxford University Press is a department of the University of Oxford.
It furthers the University's objective of excellence in research, scholarship,
and education by publishing worldwide in
Oxford   New York

Auckland   Cape Town   Dar es Salaam   Hong Kong   Karachi
Kuala Lumpur   Madrid   Melbourne   Mexico City   Nairobi
New Delhi   Shanghai   Taipei   Toronto

With offices in

Argentina   Austria   Brazil   Chile   Czech Republic   France   Greece
Guatemala   Hungary   Italy   Japan   Poland   Portugal   Singapore
South Korea   Switzerland   Thailand   Turkey   Ukraine   Vietnam

Oxford is a registered trade mark of Oxford University Press
in the UK and in certain other countries

Database right Oxford University Press (maker)

This book first published 2010

Winnie's Midnight Dragon first published 2006
Happy Birthday, Winnie! first published 2007
Winnie's Flying Carpet first published 2008

The stories are complete and unabridged

2 4 6 8 10 9 7 5 3 1

British Library Cataloguing in Publication Data
Data available

ISBN: 978-0-19-272991-0

Printed in Singapore

Paper used in the production of this book is a natural,
recyclable product made from wood grown in sustainable forests.
The manufacturing process conforms to the environmental
regulations of the country of origin

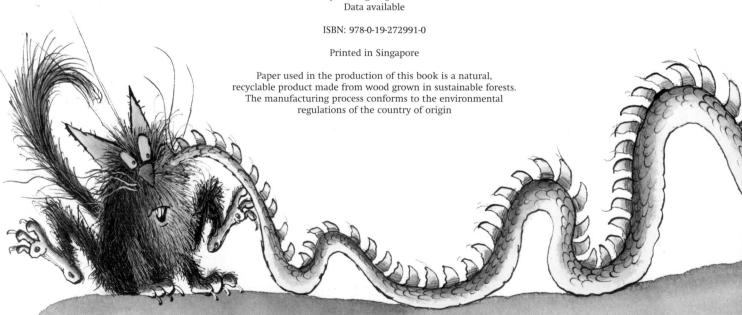

www.korkypaul.com

Winnie's
Midnight Dragon

'Time for bed,' said Winnie the Witch,
as the clock struck twelve.
Witches always go to bed at midnight.
Winnie turned off the lights and went upstairs.

She brushed her teeth, washed her face,
put on her nightie and climbed into bed.
In two minutes she was snoring.

Wilbur, her big black cat, was already asleep.
He was curled up in his basket, dreaming.

Two minutes later, Wilbur woke up.
He could hear a funny noise in the garden.

He crept to the cat flap and peeped out.
There was something on the door mat.
Something with big green eyes.

'Meeoww!' cried Wilbur
and he jumped back.
A long nose poked
through the cat flap.

Then there was a puff of smoke.
The cat flap wobbled and shook.

A spiky body, then a long tail, followed the nose.
There was a baby dragon in Winnie's house!
'Meeoww!' cried Wilbur. He turned three
backward somersaults and ran into the hall.

The baby dragon thought this was fun.
He ran after Wilbur.
Swish, swish went his tail.
Winnie's grandfather clock wobbled and shook.

DING! DONG! BOING!

'Meeoww!' cried Wilbur and he raced upstairs.
The baby dragon ran after him.
Swish, swish went his tail.
Winnie's suit of armour wobbled
and shook and rolled down the stairs.

CRASH! BANG! CLANG!

'Meeoww!' cried Wilbur outside Winnie's door.
Winnie woke up and jumped out of bed.
'Whatever's that?' she said.

Then she saw a puff of smoke coming
from behind her broomstick.
'Oh no!' said Winnie. 'My broomstick is on fire!'

Winnie grabbed her broomstick.
'Goodness gracious me!' said Winnie.
'It's a baby dragon! He could burn my house down.
We'll have to find his mother, Wilbur.'

'Where's your mother, little dragon?'
Winnie asked.
'Boo hoo hoo,' cried the baby dragon.

A cloud of smoke came out of his nose.
Puff, puff.

Then Winnie had an idea.
She waved her magic wand three times, and shouted,

Abracadabra!

'Puff!' went the dragon,
and out of his nose came. . .

a cloud of butterflies.
'Puff, puff, puff,' went the baby dragon,
who was very surprised.

SMASH!
went Winnie's best bowl.

SPLASH!
went the vase of flowers.

There were butterflies everywhere.
Wilbur loved chasing butterflies.
The baby dragon loved chasing anything!

CRASH!
went the table.

'That wasn't such a good idea,' said Winnie.
She waved her magic wand again, and shouted,

Abracadabra!

Out of the dragon's nose came. . .
Nothing.

'Good,' said Winnie. 'Now let's get some sleep.'
But the baby dragon didn't want to sleep.
He wanted to play.

'Bother!' said Winnie.
'We'd better find your mother right now!'

She got a torch and went out onto the roof.
'Yoo hoo,' she called.

It was quiet and dark on the roof.
'Yoo hoo,' Winnie called again,
and waved her torch.

Suddenly there was a flash of fire,
and the sound of great wings.
The baby dragon jumped up and down.
'Mamamamama,' he called.
'Yoo hoo hoo!' called Winnie.

But the baby dragon's mother didn't see them.
Then Winnie had a wonderful idea.

She grabbed her wand,
waved it six times, shouted,

Abracadabra!

and there, above her house,
was an enormous moon.

The mother dragon came flying back.
She swooped down and scooped up her baby.

'Wait a minute!' called Winnie.
She waved her magic wand, and shouted,

Abracadabra!

'Puff!' went the baby dragon and smoke
came out of his nose again.

The two dragons flew high into the sky and disappeared.

Winnie waved her wand, shouted,

Abracadabra!

and the enormous moon went out.
'Now let's go back to bed, Wilbur,' she said.

Winnie climbed into bed and shut her eyes.
In half a minute she was snoring.
Wilbur was already asleep in his basket.

Just then, the sun rose. The night was over.
But Winnie the Witch and Wilbur were fast asleep.

Happy Birthday, Winnie!

When Winnie the Witch turned over the page on her calendar, she saw a big red circle around Friday the thirteenth.

'That's my birthday!' she said.
'I'll have a party this year, Wilbur.'
'Purr,' said Wilbur. He loved parties.

'What kind of party?' Winnie wondered.
'I know, a garden party.'

On Monday Winnie wrote out the invitations
and sent them by Winni-e-mail.
She invited . . .

Aunty Alice,
Uncle Owen,
her three sisters Wanda, Wilma and Wendy,
all of her friends,
and Cousin Cuthbert.

On Tuesday she made herself a party dress,
and a matching bow for Wilbur.
'Purr,' said Wilbur. I look lovely, he thought.

On Wednesday Winnie made lots and lots of food.
Wilbur helped.

Thursday was the day to get the garden ready.
Winnie went outside. It looked rather scruffy.
Then Winnie had a very good idea.
She took out her wand, waved it, shouted,

Abracadabra!

And the garden was ready for the party.
'That was easy,' Winnie said.

'Now what else? Oh yes, I need a surprise.
A good party always has a surprise.
I'll have to think about that.'

Friday the thirteenth was a lovely sunny day,
which was lucky.

At two o'clock Winnie's guests arrived.
'Happy birthday, Winnie,' they shouted,
and they piled up the presents on the lawn.

Wanda, Wilma and Wendy gave
Winnie a magic carpet.
She'd always wanted one of those.

Uncle Owen gave her
a bat in a cage.
She'd never wanted one of those.

Aunty Alice gave her a Book
of Special Spells,

and there was a magic trumpet
from Cousin Cuthbert.

'Let's play some games!' Winnie said.
First they played musical broomsticks.
That was fun, but there was a lot of pushing.
Uncle Owen pushed Aunty Alice into a prickle bush. Ouch!

Cousin Cuthbert bounced off a broomstick and landed in the fountain. So they let him win.

'Now we'll have a treasure hunt,' said Winnie.

Uncle Owen looked in the maze, and got lost.

Wilma looked in the bat's cage, and the bat flew away.

Wendy looked in the bouncy castle. Bang!

Wanda found the treasure, but she had some help.

'The next game is hide-and-seek,' Winnie shouted.
But there was so much noise nobody heard her.

So Winnie picked up her new magic trumpet.
Toot, toot, toot,
Winnie tootled . . .

and **everybody** disappeared.
Winnie was surprised.

Then she was cross.
Where had they gone?

Winnie looked
in the maze.

Nobody.

She looked in the
bat's cage.

Nothing.

She looked in the
bouncy castle.

Nobody.

'Blithering broomsticks!' Winnie said.
'Who will eat all my lovely food?'

Then Winnie saw a label on the trumpet.

IMPORTANT:
to make people disappear, toot three times
to make them come back, stand on your head
and toot three times

So Winnie stood on her head.
Toot, toot, toot,
she tootled . . .

and everybody came back, feeling hungry.
They ate up all the food.

'And now it's time for the surprise,' said Winnie.
She opened her new Book of Special Spells.
'Shut your eyes and think about your
favourite cake!' she said.

Everybody shut their eyes.
Aunty Alice thought about chocolate cake.
Uncle Owen thought about fruit cake.
Cousin Cuthbert thought about rainbow cake.
Wilbur thought about cheesecake.
He loved cheesecake.

Then Winnie the Witch shut her eyes,
turned around three times, stamped her foot,
waved her wand, and shouted,

Abracadabra!

And there was the biggest birthday cake
in the whole world,
with candles on the top.

There was a layer of chocolate cake,
a layer of fruit cake,
a layer of rainbow cake,
a layer of cheesecake.
There was strawberry shortcake,
ginger sponge cake,
orange cake,
Black Forest cake.

'How will you blow out the candles?'
asked Cousin Cuthbert.
'That's easy,' Winnie said . . .

and she rode on her magic carpet to the top of the cake.
Puff, puff, puuffffffff!

'Ha ha ha,' laughed Winnie.
'This party is such fun, Wilbur!
I'm a very lucky witch.'

Wilbur didn't say anything.
His mouth was full of cheesecake.
What a lucky black cat!

Happy Birthday to you!

Winnie's Flying Carpet

Winnie the Witch was busy
writing letters.

They were thank-you letters
for her birthday presents.

Now there was only one left, the trickiest letter.
Winnie's sisters, Wilma, Wanda, and Wendy,
had given her a flying carpet.
Winnie had always wanted a flying carpet.
But *this* flying carpet had been a disappointment.

Actually, it had been a disaster.

Dear Wilma,

Wanda, and Wendy,

thank you very much

for the

There was the time it got tangled
in Winnie's washing.

And the day it tipped over as they were passing a duck pond.

And then one day it turned a corner too quickly.

After that, Winnie rolled up the carpet, tied it with string . . .

put it in the broom cupboard, and locked the door.

But Winnie wanted to write something *nice* about the carpet in her thank-you letter.

She unlocked the cupboard, untied the carpet, and spread it on the armchair.

It is a beautiful carpet, she thought. It seems a pity not to use it.

So Winnie decided to give it one more chance.

Just then, the door bell rang.

Ding! Dong!

Winnie hurried off to answer it . . .

just as Wilbur came inside.

After a busy morning climbing trees
and chasing butterflies, he was ready
for a sleep.

The sun was shining on the flying carpet.
It looked so warm and comfortable.
Wilbur jumped up and in one minute
he was snoring.

The flying carpet waited
one more minute.

Then it rose gently into the air.
Wilbur didn't wake up.

It flew gently around the room.
Wilbur didn't wake up.

Then it zoomed out of the window.
Wilbur woke up.

'Meeoow!' he cried.

Winnie heard him.
She looked up, just in time to see the
flying carpet zoom up into the sky.

'Oh no!' cried Winnie. She grabbed her magic
wand and her broomstick, and zoomed up
into the sky after them.

Winnie flew as fast as her broomstick
could go, but the carpet was faster.
It swooped over the clock tower,
and under a bridge.

Winnie followed it.
'Hang on tight, Wilbur!' she called.
'Meeoow!' cried Wilbur.

Then the carpet flew over a funfair.
What fun!

First it whizzed down the
Roller Coaster Rocket.
Winnie whizzed down behind it.

Then it tried the
Terrible Twister.

The flying carpet was
having a wonderful time.
Wilbur was having a
horrible time.

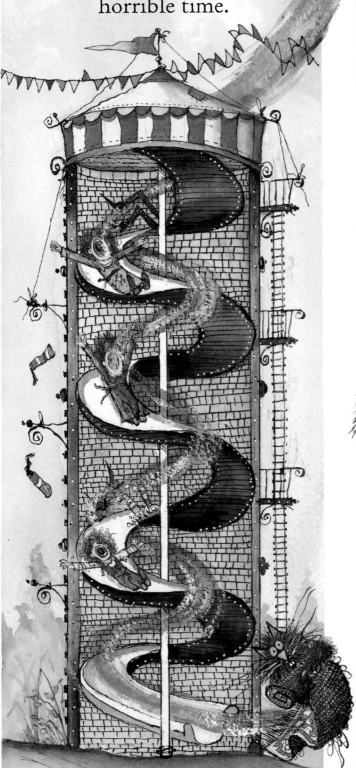

Winnie was worried.
She would never catch them.

Then she had an idea.
She waved her magic wand,
shouted,

Abracadabra!

. . . and everything stopped.

Nothing whizzed or zoomed
or shrieked or splashed.

All was still. Including the flying carpet.

Wilbur jumped onto Winnie's shoulder.
'Purr, purr,' he said.

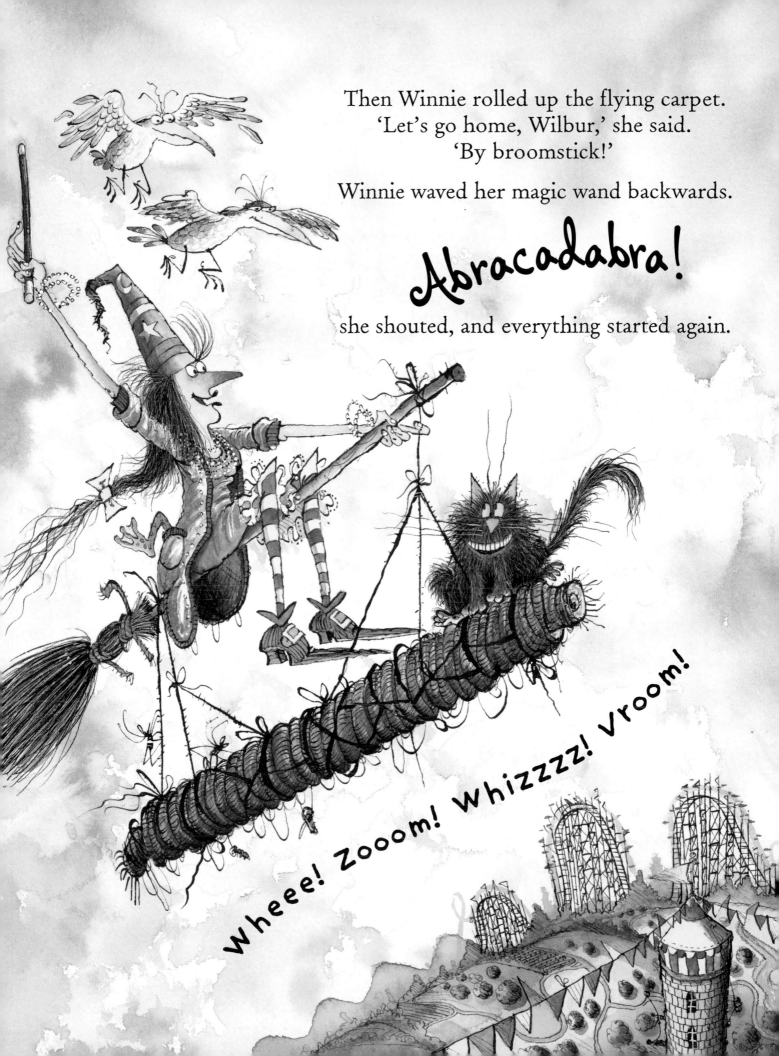

Then Winnie rolled up the flying carpet.
'Let's go home, Wilbur,' she said.
'By broomstick!'

Winnie waved her magic wand backwards.

Abracadabra!

she shouted, and everything started again.

Wheee! Zooom! Whizzzz! Vroom!

Winnie and Wilbur landed in Winnie's garden.
Winnie frowned at the flying carpet.

What would she do with it?

Then Winnie had a wonderful idea.
She shut her eyes,
waved her wand, shouted,

. . . and there, tied to two trees, was a beautiful hammock.

Winnie and Wilbur climbed in. They were both very tired.

The hammock rocked gently in the breeze.

'This is so comfortable, Wilbur,'
said Winnie.

But Wilbur didn't hear her.
He was already fast asleep